# IT HAPPENS TO THE BEST OF

The six players below are in the Hall of Fame, but here are some career records they wish they hadn't set:

- Hank Aaron — hit into 328 double plays
- Lou Brock — was thrown out stealing 307 times
- Reggie Jackson — struck out 2,597 times
- Nap Lajoie — once committed five errors in one game
- Cy Young — lost 316 games, the most by any pitcher ever
- Brooks Robinson — hit into a record four triple plays

Get the lowdown on the most amazing moments and funniest facts in baseball's batty history. It's all here in

# SEVENTH-INNING STRETCH:
## Time-out for Baseball Trivia

# Seventh-Inning Stretch:

## Time-out for Baseball Trivia

by Brad Herzog

NATIONAL BASEBALL LIBRARY, COOPERSTOWN, NY

**A *Sports Illustrated For Kids* Book**

BANTAM BOOKS

TORONTO • NEW YORK • LONDON • SYDNEY • AUCKLAND

SEVENTH-INNING STRETCH: Time-out for Baseball Trivia by Brad Herzog

A Bantam Book/May 1994

Sports Illustrated For Kids and **KiDS** are registered trademarks of Time Inc.
Sports Illustrated For Kids Books are published in cooperation with Bantam
Doubleday Dell Publishing Group, Inc. under license from Time Inc.

Cover and interior design by Miriam Dustin

For information address: Bantam Books

ISBN 0-553-48162-2

Published simultaneously in the United States and Canada

Bantam books are published by Bantam Books, a division of Bantam Doubleday
Dell Publishing Group, Inc. Its trademark, consisting of the words "Bantam
Books" and the portrayal of a rooster, is Registered in the U.S. Patent and
Trademark Office and in other countries. Marca Registrada. Bantam Books, 1540
Broadway, New York, NY 10036

Printed in the United States of America

CWO 0 9 8 7 6 5 4 3 2 1

Cover photo credits: top, Ronald C. Modra/Sports Illustrated; middle, Manny
Millan/Sports Illustrated; bottom, National Baseball Library, Cooperstown, NY.

# INTRODUCTION

Catch up on more than 90 years of baseball's battiest history! *SEVENTH-INNING STRETCH: Time-out for Baseball Trivia* will take you from the first organized major league game to last year's no-hitters, from the All-Star Game to the World Series, and from the age of Babe Ruth to the days of Barry Bonds. Each of the three sections covers a part of baseball's past. You'll read about baseball's big boppers and biggest bloopers and laugh about the craziest names and wildest games. There are even puzzles for you to do along the way. So buckle up for a trip through time — the national pastime, that is. ***Play ball!***

WILLIE MAYS

# 1846

# THE FIRST GAME

For many years, people believed that baseball was invented by a Civil War general named Abner Doubleday in 1839 in Cooperstown, New York. Today, however, most historians believe that a man named Alexander Cartwright invented the game that has become America's national pastime.

The first game played under Cartwright's rules occurred on June 19, 1846, in the town of Hoboken, New Jersey. Cartwright's team, the Knickerbockers (pictured below, in 1864), took on a team called the New York Nine. Despite the fact that Cartwright had invented the game and umpired the first contest, his team lost, 23-1!

NATIONAL BASEBALL LIBRARY, COOPERSTOWN, NY

# BASEBALL'S BEGINNINGS

## THREE FINGER BROWN

His real name was Mordecai Peter Centennial Brown, but everybody knew him as "Three Finger." That's because he lost most of his index finger and mangled his middle finger in a childhood accident. Yet Three Finger Brown became one of the greatest pitchers of his time, winning 239 games from 1903-1916. Many people believe that because his middle finger was bent his curveball curved even more!

## 1903 ➤ THE FIRST WORLD SERIES

The National League (which had begun in 1876) and American League owners didn't get along when the A.L. was first created in 1901, but two years later the owners of the first-place teams in each of the two leagues decided to see which team was the best. That's how the World Series was born.

The first World Series, between the Boston Pilgrims and the Pittsburgh Pirates in 1903, was a best-of-nine contest. The first team to win five games (it was Boston) won the Series. The following year, in 1904, the two leagues could not agree to play, so there was no World Series. But since 1905, there has been a "Fall Classic" after every regular season.

## THE BIGGEST FAN

The lowest recorded attendance for a professional baseball game occurred on the cold and rainy afternoon of November 8, 1905. Two minor league teams, the Oakland Oaks and Portland Beavers, had each already been eliminated from the playoffs. So how many fans paid to watch the game that day? One!

## BIG BLOOPER

On September 23, 1908, New York Giants first baseman Fred Merkle, starting in his first game, made a mistake that cost his team an important win. He became known forever after as "Bonehead" Merkle.

The Giants were playing the Cubs in New York that day, tied for first place. With the score at 1-1, with two out in the bottom of the ninth inning and a man on first, Fred hit a single, sending the runner at first to third base.

The next batter, Al Bridwell, slapped a single, and the man on third base scored what seemed to be the winning run. The New York fans poured onto the field, thinking the Giants had won the game. Fred, who had been on first base, decided to run into the dugout instead of running to second base. He didn't think he had to tag second because the winning run had scored.

Johnny Evers, the Cubs' second baseman, got the ball and stepped on second base. The umpire wasn't sure whether to call Fred out or to say that the Giants won had the game, so he went home! At ten o'clock that night, he finally made his decision — Fred was out, and the game was still tied!

The Giants and the Cubs ended the regular season with the same record — 98 wins and 55 losses. The teams played

## TY COBB

Ty Cobb was generally regarded as one of the meanest players in baseball history, spiking any second or third baseman who got in his way. But he was also one of the best. After batting only .240 his rookie year, the Detroit Tigers outfielder hit over .300 in each of the next 23 seasons. His .367 lifetime batting average and 2,245 runs are records that may never be broken. No other player has ever won more than eight batting crowns in his career, but the "Georgia Peach" won 12, including nine in a row!

one game to decide the pennant, and the Cubs won it. So by not tagging second base, Fred Merkle may have cost the Giants the pennant!

## CY VERSUS CY

In major league history, there have been 21 pitchers named Cy. If you take 20 of them and combine all their wins, they add up to 460 victories. The other Cy was Cy Young. He pitched for 22 seasons in the majors (1890-1911) and collected 511 wins, a record that may stand forever.

### 1913  ACT YOUR AGE

Merito Acosta appeared in nine games as an outfielder for the Washington Senators in 1913. He was only 17 years old, yet he hit .300 in 20 at-bats with four walks, three runs scored, two steals, and a triple. He also became the youngest player in American League history to get a pinch hit.

## Wacky Fact

On July 17, 1914, New York Giant outfielder Red Murray was struck by lightning after catching a fly ball!

### 1917  NO-HIT MAGIC

On June 23, 1917, Babe Ruth, who began his baseball career as a pitcher, was starting for the Boston Red Sox. Babe walked the first batter of the game, Eddie Foster, but he didn't like the calls the umpire had made. So Babe made a big mistake — he slugged the umpire! Naturally, he was ejected from the game.

A player named Ernie Shore came into the game as an emergency relief pitcher and picked off Foster, who was attempting to steal. Ernie then retired the next 26 batters in order. As a result, Ruth "pitched in" for what turned out to be a no-hitter!

## 1919 ▷ THE BLACK SOX SCANDAL

One of the darkest chapters in baseball history occurred in 1919. The World Series between the Chicago White Sox and the Cincinnati Reds was not expected to be close. The White Sox had won 88 games that year and were considered baseball's best team.

Though Chicago wound up winning three games, Cincinnati won the World Series. The best team in baseball hadn't played very well.

Later, the world found out why. Ed Cicotte, the losing pitcher in Game 1, admitted that gamblers had offered him and seven other players money to lose the World Series. A total of $100,000 dollars was offered to them, which was a lot of money to baseball players in those days.

The eight players were tried and found innocent in court, but Kenesaw Mountain Landis, the commissioner of baseball, still banned them from baseball. Judge Landis believed he had to keep gambling as far away from baseball as possible, or fans would wonder if their favorite players were really trying.

Two of the eight "Black Sox" who were kicked out of baseball had played well in the World Series. Buck Weaver, the third baseman, batted .324 with four doubles, four runs, and no errors. He said that he had never accepted the money and maintained that he was innocent until the day he died.

# WALTER JOHNSON

Walter Johnson was the Nolan Ryan of his day. He spent 21 seasons as a pitcher for the Washington Senators, and won 416 games, a total second only to Cy Young's 511 victories. He also led the league in strikeouts 12 times and threw a record 110 shutouts. The Senators usually finished low in the standings. But in 1924, Walter's golden right arm finally led the Senators to a World Series championship! That season the "Big Train" led the league in wins, earned run average, strikeouts, and shutouts.

The other player who played well in the Series was one of the best ever to play baseball. His name was "Shoeless" Joe Jackson. Shoeless Joe had the highest batting average in the Series (.375) and hit the only home run. He also had the third highest lifetime batting average of all time (.356). Yet Shoeless Joe was still banned from baseball, and because of that he hasn't been elected to the Hall of Fame.

## 1920 ▷ WORLD SERIES MOMENT

Bill Wambsganss, whose last name was so long it often appeared as just "Wamby" in the boxscores, was not a very well-known player in his day. But he still holds a special place in baseball history.

It was October 10, 1920, and Bill and his Cleveland Indian teammates were playing the Brooklyn Dodgers in Game 5 of the World Series.

Brooklyn had men on first and second. The next batter stepped up to the plate and hit a liner to Wamby at second base. He caught it on the fly, stepped on second base—catching the runner off—and tagged the base runner coming from first base for the only unassisted triple play in World Series history!

## NUTTY NICKNAMES

| | |
|---|---|
| George Kelly (1915-1932) | "Highpockets" |
| Burleigh Grimes (1916-1934) | "Ol' Stubblebeard" |
| Nick Cullop (1926-1931) | "Tomato Face" |
| Sammy Byrd (1929-1936) | "Babe Ruth's Legs" |

## DAFFY DEAL

How did Oyster Joe Martina, a so-so pitcher for the

1924 Washington Sentors, get his nickname? It wasn't because he liked shellfish, but because he was traded from Dallas to New Orleans for two barrels of oysters when he was a minor league pitcher in 1921!

 **1924**     **BIG BLOOPER**

Catcher Hank Gowdy had been the hero of the 1914 World Series when he batted .545 with the Boston Braves. But 10 years later, the shoe was on the other foot.

Hank's team, the New York Giants, was playing the Washington Senators in the seventh game of the 1924 World Series. The score was tied, 3-3, in the bottom of the 12th inning when Muddy Ruel, a weak hitter, stepped up to the plate for the Senators.

Muddy swung and lofted a high pop fly straight up in the air. Hank pulled off his catcher's mask and threw it aside. Suddenly, the wind blew the ball back to where Hank had tossed his mask. Just as the ball was coming down, Hank stepped right onto his mask . . . and his foot got stuck!

As he tried to shake free, he tripped and fell, missing the ball entirely. Given a second chance, Muddy slapped a double down the leftfield line. Minutes later, he scored the winning run, and once again the New York Giants had lost a big game because of a big blooper.

**1925**     **ACT YOUR AGE**

Jimmie Foxx was a 17-year-old catcher with the Philadelphia Athletics in 1925. In only nine at-bats that year, he got six hits! Soon "Double X" (Jimmie's nickname) became a first baseman. In fact, with a .325 lifetime batting average and 534 home runs, he is considered one of the great first basemen of all time.

## K-SMART

Who was the toughest man to strike out in baseball history? Ty Cobb? Joe DiMaggio? Willie Mays? Nope. His name was Joe Sewell. Joe was a shortstop for the Cleveland Indians and New York Yankees for 14 years, and in that time, he had 7,132 official at-bats and struck out *only* 114 times.

How good was Joe's eye at the plate? Look at the record for the most strikeouts by a batter in one season. Bobby Bonds (Barry Bonds's father) set the record in 1970 by striking out 189 times.

## KINGS OF THE HILL

Exactly 20 pitchers in major league history have won 300 or more games in their careers, a feat that is just about as difficult as reaching 3,000 hits. Here's a list of the pitchers with the top ten win totals and their records:

|  | Wins | Losses |
|---|---|---|
| Cy Young | 511 | 316 |
| Walter Johnson | 416 | 279 |
| Christy Mathewson | 373 | 188 |
| Grover Alexander | 373 | 208 |
| Warren Spahn | 363 | 245 |
| Kid Nichols | 361 | 208 |
| Pud Galvin | 361 | 308 |
| Tim Keefe | 342 | 225 |
| Steve Carlton | 329 | 244 |

That means, Bobby struck out almost twice as many times in *one* season as Joe struck out in his entire 14-year career!

In 1925, Joe had 608 official at-bats, but he struck out only four times. Many players have struck out four times in one game!

## ONE-MAN TEAM

By hitting 54 home runs in 1920 and 60 home runs in 1927, Babe Ruth hit more home runs than any other *team* in the American League in each of those years!

## HOW TO FIGURE... BATTING AVERAGE

A batting average is how many hits a player gets divided by how many times the player had a chance to bat. For example, if someone had three hits in nine at-bats, you divide three by nine.

**3 divided by 9 = .333**

... so the person has a batting average of .333.

Three hits in nine at-bats is the same as 200 hits in 600 at-bats:

**200 divided by 600 = .333**

Any batting average over .300 is very good, and Ty Cobb's lifetime batting average of .367 is the best ever. In his best season, he had 248 hits in 591 at-bats. What was his batting average? (Answer on page 76.)

**248 divided by 591 = _____**

## BABE RUTH

Babe Ruth is the most famous baseball player ever. He showed the world the power and excitement of the home run. And by hitting homers, Babe made the game more fun for the fans. People filled the seats wherever he played, and he kept people interested in baseball at a time when fans were still getting over the Black Sox Scandal.

Babe hit 54 homers in 1920, and 59 in 1921. Six years later, he hit 60 homers, a record that lasted for 34 years until Roger Maris broke it in 1961.

Babe finished his career with a .342 lifetime batting average and the highest slugging percentage (.690) in baseball history. He holds the record for most career walks (2,056), and he's second in runs scored (2,174) and runs batted in (2,211). Only Hank Aaron hit more home runs (755) than Babe's total of 714.

1927 ▷ **STRAIGHT A'S**

The 1927 Yankees are considered by many people to be the greatest team in baseball history. They won 110 games, swept the World Series and had five future Hall of Famers on the team. But it was the American League's second-place team in 1927, the Philadelphia A's, that was made up of a record seven future Hall of Famers!

Three of them — Ty Cobb, Eddie Collins, and Zack Wheat — were closing out their awesome careers. The other four — Lefty Grove, Jimmie Foxx, Al Simmons and Mickey Cochrane — were just beginning what would be brilliant careers.

## OH, BROTHER!

Paul and Lloyd Waner were teammates on the Pittsburgh Pirates for 14 seasons, from 1927 through 1940. Paul, the older brother, was called "Big Poison." Lloyd's nickname, of course, became "Little Poison."

In 1927, the Waner brothers combined for possibly the best season ever by a pair of siblings. Together, they produced a .367 batting average, 460 hits, and 246 runs. Paul led the league in hits, while Lloyd led the league in runs.

The Waner brothers, who combined for 5,611 career hits, are the only brothers to be both elected to the Baseball Hall of Fame.

# EXTRA INNINGS

Here are some questions to see how how much baseball history you've "caught" so far! Check your score on page 72 to see if you are an MVP or a minor leaguer!

**1.** The first World Series was played in 1903. Since then, one team has won more World Series than any other. Do you know which team it is?

**2.** Cy Young holds the major league record of 511 career victories as a pitcher, but do you know who has lost more games (316) than any other pitcher in history?

**3.** "Shoeless" Joe Jackson was banned from baseball in 1920 because of his involvement with gamblers during the 1919 World Series. Nearly 70 years later, another all-time great was banned from baseball because of his relationship with gambling. Who is he?

**4.** Walter Johnson pitched for a team that moved from its original city and is now called the Minnesota Twins. What team was it?

# HALL OF FAME FILL-IN

These 22 players got into the Hall of Fame but can you get them into this fill-in? They are divided up according to the number of letters in their last names. Your job is to figure out where their **last names** fit. Two names are already done for you and make good places to start. Have a ball with the guys from the Hall! (Check your answers on page 73.)

**3 letters**
Mel OTT

**4 letters**
Whitey FORD
Jimmie FOXX
Willie MAYS
Babe RUTH

**5 letters**
Hank AARON
Ernie BANKS
Johnny BENCH
Rod CAREW
Ralph KINER
Warren SPAHN

**6 letters**
Sandy KOUFAX
Mickey MANTLE
Goose GOSLIN

**7 letters**
Rogers HORNSBY

**8 letters**
Roberto CLEMENTE
Joe DIMAGGIO
Willie STARGELL
Ted WILLIAMS

**9 letters**
Hank GREENBERG
Harmon KILLEBREW
Christy MATHEWSON

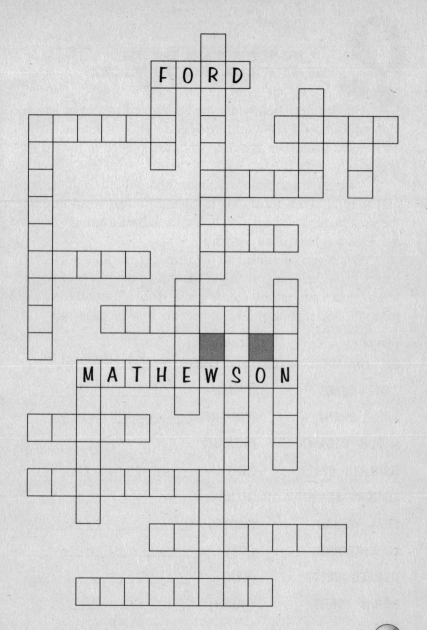

FORD

MATHEWSON

# SIBLING SCRAMBLE

Oh Brother! Below are the scrambled names of seven Hall of Fame players and three future Hall of Famers who each had a brother or brothers who also played in the major leagues.

Unscramble the player's name and write it in the space on the right. Then locate the last names in the word find on the next page, going up, down, forward, backward, or diagonal. One has been done for you.

When you've circled all the names, write all the leftover letters from the grid (starting at the top of the grid and going left to right and top to bottom) in the spaces below the puzzle to see the secret phrase! (Check your answers on page 74.)

| Player | Brother | |
|---|---|---|
| OJE MIGIADOG | (DOM and VINCE) | Joe   DiMaggio |
| ZIDYZ ENAD | (PAUL) | _____ _____ |
| KAHN ROANA | (TOMMIE) | _____ _____ |
| SHOUN REGAWN | (ALBERT) | _____ _____ |
| DOGLAYR PRYER | (JIM) | _____ _____ |
| TISHCRY SHAMTENOW | (HENRY) | _____ _____ |
| LUPA WERAN | (LLOYD) | _____ _____ |
| LIPH KROINE | (JOE) | _____ _____ |
| OGREEG BETTR | (KEN) | _____ _____ |
| BORIN YONUT | (LARRY) | _____ _____ |

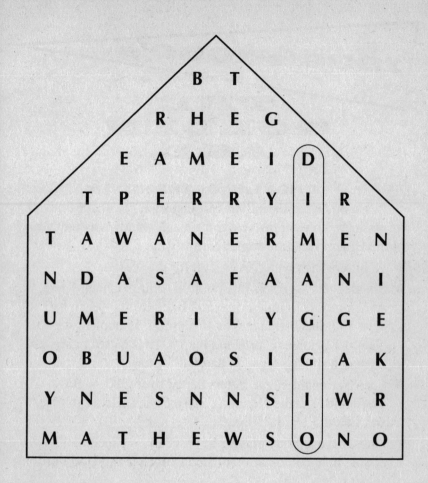

```
          B   T
          R   H   E   G
      E   A   M   E   I   D
      T   P   E   R   R   Y   I   R
  T   A   W   A   N   E   R   M   E   N
  N   D   A   S   A   F   A   A   N   I
  U   M   E   R   I   L   Y   G   G   E
  O   B   U   A   O   S   I   G   A   K
  Y   N   E   S   N   N   S   I   W   R
  M   A   T   H   E   W   S   O   N   O
```

**SECRET PHRASE:**

\_\_ \_\_ \_\_  \_\_ \_\_ \_\_ \_\_ \_\_  \_\_ \_\_

\_\_ \_\_  \_\_ \_\_ \_\_ \_\_ \_\_ \_\_ \_\_

\_\_ \_\_ \_\_ \_\_ \_\_ \_\_ \_\_ \_\_ \_\_ \_\_ .

# THE GOLDEN AGE

## 1930 ▷ THE YEAR OF THE HITTER

No other season in baseball history quite matches 1930 for its incredible offensive explosion. It's known as the Year of the Hitter. Here are some reasons why:

- 98 hitters each batted over .300 for the season.
- Six sluggers — Hack Wilson, Lou Gehrig, Chuck Klein, Al Simmons, Jimmie Foxx, and Babe Ruth — each had at least 150 runs batted in. Hack Wilson's 56 homers were a National League record, and his 190 runs batted in are the most in a single season in baseball history.
- Four National League hitters batted over .380 — Bill Terry (.401), Babe Herman (.393), Chuck Klein (.386), and Lefty O'Doul (.383).
- Only two everyday players in baseball — Cincinnati's double play combination of Leo Durocher and Hod Ford — hit below .250.
- Pitcher Guy Bush of the Cubs gave up 155 runs that season, a modern National League record!

## 1933 ▷ A STAR IS BORN

The first All-Star Game was held on July 6, 1933, at Comiskey Park in Chicago. The American League won the game, 4-2, thanks to the oldest player on the field — 38-year-old Babe Ruth. Babe hit a two-run home run in the third inning, the first homer in All-Star history.

## 1934 ▷ OH, BROTHER!

In 1934, the St. Louis Cardinals had two pitchers who were brothers. They were named Jay and Paul Dean. Jay was called "Dizzy," and Paul was sometimes called "Daffy," but on the mound they certainly didn't goof around.

Before the season began, Dizzy boasted that he and his brother would combine to win 45 games. As it turned out, they won more than that! Dizzy won 30 games and led the league in strikeouts. Daffy won 19 games and pitched a no-hitter!

### WACKY FACT

When Babe Ruth hit the 700th home run of his career on July 13, 1934, nobody thought any player would come close to hitting 700 home runs again. At the time, Lou Gehrig was second with 314 career homers, followed by Rogers Hornsby with 301.

Hank Aaron, the man who later became the home run king, was just five months old in July 1934.

### ACT YOUR AGE

Cleveland Indians pitcher Bob Feller had quite a rookie year as a 17-year-old in 1936. On August 23, in his first big league start, Bob gave up only six hits and struck out 15 batters. On September 13, Bob set a new American League record by striking out 17 batters — and becoming the only player in baseball history to match his age in strikeouts in one game!

**1938** ▷ **NO-HIT MAGIC**

Johnny Vander Meer was a lefthanded pitcher for the Cincinnati Reds. On June 11 and June 15, 1938, he did what no one else has ever done. He pitched two no-hitters in a row!

Johnny's second straight no-hitter, four days after his first, was the first night game ever held at Brooklyn's Ebbets Field. That probably made it easier for the pitchers because the hitters had trouble seeing the ball.

Despite being the only major leaguer ever to toss two straight no-hitters, Johnny Vander Meer wound up losing more games in his career than he won.

## Wacky Fact

Walter Alston batted only once — for the St. Louis Cardinals in 1936 — and he struck out. Yet he's in the Hall of Fame! Why? Because he later managed the Dodgers for 23 years (from 1954 to 1976), winning more than 2,000 games and four World Series.

**1940** ▷ **MORE NO-HIT MAGIC**

By the time he was 21 years old in 1940, Cleveland Indian pitcher Bob Feller had already led the American League in wins, complete games, strikeouts, and innings pitched. He had thrown three one-hitters, but had yet to toss

# LOU GEHRIG

Lou Gehrig's nickname was "The Iron Horse" because from 1925 to 1939 he didn't miss one game. His record of 2,130 consecutive games played is one of the awesome feats in sports. Lou hit 493 career home runs and had a lifetime batting average of .340. He holds the A.L. records for RBIs in a season with 184 and most grand slams in a career with 23.

Lou retired from baseball early in 1939 when doctors discovered that he had a fatal disease called amyotrophic lateral sclerosis, which affects the spinal cord and causes muscle weakness. Today, it is commonly known as "Lou Gehrig's Disease."

NATIONAL BASEBALL LIBRARY, COOPERSTOWN, NY

On July 4, 1939, 61,808 fans at Yankee Stadium celebrated Lou Gehrig Day. Lou told the fans, "Today, I consider myself the luckiest man on the face of the earth." He would die two years later at the age of 37.

a no-hitter.

On Opening Day in 1940, however, it happened. Bob no-hit the Chicago White Sox, 1-0, for the only Opening Day no-hitter in league history.

## 1941 JOE'S AND TED'S EXCELLENT ADVENTURES

Two of baseball's greatest hitters were Joe DiMaggio and Ted Williams. DiMaggio played centerfield for the New York Yankees from 1936 to 1951, and Williams played left-field for the Boston Red Sox from

## HOW TO FIGURE... EARNED RUN AVERAGE

An earned run average is a measure of how many runs a pitcher allows per game. Since there are nine innings in a game, the ERA tell us how many runs the pitcher gives up for every nine innings he pitches. If, for example, a pitcher allows three earned runs in nine innings, his earned run average is 3.00.

A pitcher's ERA is figured by taking the number of earned runs he gives up, multiplying it by nine, and then dividing it by the number of innings he has pitched. For instance, if a pitcher has allowed 45 runs in 100 innings, his ERA is

**45 multiplied by nine = 405,**
**405 divided by 100 = 4.05**

In 1952, Virgil Trucks allowed 87 runs in 197 innings. What was his earned run average? (Answer on page 76.)

**87 multiplied by nine = 783,**
**783 divided by 197 = _____**

1939 to 1960. Both are now in the Hall of Fame, and in 1941, both sluggers performed feats that may never be matched again. Read on . . .

## . . . THE STREAK

On May 15, 1941, Joe got a hit against the Chicago White Sox, and he didn't stop hitting for the next two months.

In every game, "Joltin'" Joe had at least one hit. Sometimes he would get lucky, reaching base on a bad-hop single or an infield hit, but most of the time he pounded the ball. On July 2, he hit a home run to continue his hitting streak. The home run broke Wee Willie Keeler's 44-year-old record of 44 straight games with a hit.

The streak kept going and going . . . finally ending at 56 games on July 17 only because Cleveland third baseman Ken Keltner made two terrific plays to rob Joe of hits.

Joe's streak put the Yankees in first place and helped him win the American League MVP Award. It also made "56" a legendary number in the world of baseball.

## . . . THE LAST .400 HITTER

Joe DiMaggio won the MVP Award in 1941, but he wasn't the best hitter that season. That honor belonged to Ted Williams.

Ted had a .436 batting average midway through the season, but he began to slump a bit. On the very last day of the season, his batting average was just barely .400, and the Red Sox were scheduled to play a doubleheader.

Instead of playing it safe and sitting out the games to keep his average at .400, Ted played both games of the doubleheader. He got six hits in eight at-bats to raise his average to .406! It's been more than 50 years, and Ted Williams is still the last player to bat .400 in the major leagues.

## ACT YOUR AGE

Due to the shortage of major league-caliber athletes during World War II, players like Joe Nuxhall got a chance to start their baseball careers early. In 1944, Joe became the youngest player ever to participate in a major league game. In June of that year, he pitched for the Cincinnati Reds — at the age of 15 years, 10 months, and 11 days!

### NUTTY NICKNAMES

| | |
|---|---|
| Luke Appling (1930-1950) | "Old Aches and Pains" |
| Ted Williams (1939-1960) | "The Splendid Splinter" |
| Dom DiMaggio (1940-1953) | "The Little Professor" |
| Hank Arft (1948-1952) | "Bow Wow" |

### NAME GAME

Throughout baseball history, there have many players who were very good at drawing a walk. From Babe Ruth and Ted Williams to Rickey Henderson and Frank Thomas, the base on balls has been more than a pitcher's mistake. It has been an offensive weapon.

But as far as walks are concerned, there is no bigger name than Eddie. That's Eddie

## WaCKy FaCT

In 1941, Cleveland shortstop Jackie Price took batting practice at spring training while hanging up side down!

## JACKIE ROBINSON

In 1947, Jackie Robinson became the first African-American player to play in the major leagues. At the time, blacks played in separate baseball leagues called the Negro Leagues, and many ignorant people wanted it to stay that way. When Jackie played for the Brooklyn Dodgers that year, it was the beginning of the desegregation of baseball.

Though fans and fellow players shouted racist taunts at him, Jackie became a star, and brought an aggressive, running style to the game. He was National League Rookie of the Year in his first season, and batted .342 to win the N.L. Most Valuable Player Award two years later. He had shown that prejudice is wrong, in the sports world *and* the real world.

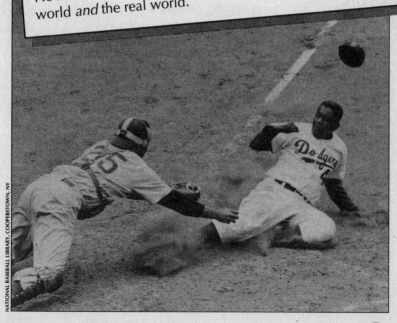

Collins, Eddie Mathews, Eddie Joost, Eddie Stanky, and Eddie Yost.

The five Eddies — sounds like a rock group — combined for a career total of 6,598 walks. Among them, they had at least 100 walks in a season a total of 27 times. In fact, four of them — all but Eddie Collins — played at about the same time. So you could call the 1940's, 1950's, and 1960's the Eddie Years.

Oh, you can add one more to the list. In 1951, St. Louis Browns owner Bill Veeck played a joke by sending a midget up to pinch-hit during a game. The 3' 7" player had such a small strike zone that he walked on four straight pitches. His name? Eddie Gaedel.

## BIG BLOOPER

On October 5, 1952, a person on the field made a mistake that may have cost the New York Yankees a victory in a World Series game. But that person wasn't a player. It was an umpire!

During the 10th inning of the fifth game between the Yankees and the Brooklyn Dodgers, New York's leadoff batter, Johnny Sain, hit a ground ball to Jackie Robinson at second, who bobbled the ball and then threw it to first base. Like many plays at first base, it was close.

Many newspapers the next day printed a large photograph of the play. The photo showed Johnny stepping on first base while the ball was still in midair. He was clearly safe, but the umpire — Art Passarella — had called him out!

The Yankees didn't score in that inning, but the Dodgers scored in the 11th inning to win the game, 6-5. As for the umpire, he was out of baseball the following year.

## WaCKy FaCT

Branch Rickey, the man who brought Jackie Robinson to the major leagues, also introduced batting helmets. His 1952 Pittsburgh Pirates team wore them, and by 1955 the whole National League was wearing them. One year later, American League players put on their helmets as well. However, if you didn't wear a batting helmet before 1956, you still didn't have to wear one!

## YOGI AND CAMPY

Two of the best catchers in major league history played at the same time in the 1950's, and now both are in the Hall of Fame. Yogi Berra and his New York Yankees faced Roy Campanella and his Brooklyn Dodgers in the World Series five times in eight seasons — in 1949, 1952, 1953, 1955, and 1956.

Yogi was named American League Most Valuable Player in 1951, 1954, and 1955. Roy, one of the first African-American players in the big leagues, was the National League MVP in 1951, 1953, and 1955. His career was cut short when he was paralyzed in a car accident in 1958.

Yogi Berra may be best known, however, for his "Yogi-isms." That is, sometimes he says things that don't make much sense. For example, when Yogi was asked about the Yankees' loss to the Pirates in the 1960 World Series, he said, "We made too many wrong mistakes." When someone asked him how he liked school when he was growing up, he answered, "Closed." Yogi also said, "A nickel ain't worth a dime anymore" and "The game's not over until it's over."

## 1956 ➤ WORLD SERIES MOMENT

Don Larsen was not the world's greatest pitcher. In 1954, he won three games and lost 21. In 1960, he won one game and lost 10. But for one game in 1956, he was perfect.

In the fifth game of the 1956 World Series, Don pitched for the New York Yankees against the Brooklyn Dodgers. He faced 27 batters without allowing one of them to reach first base. It was the first perfect game since 1922 and the only perfect game in World Series history!

## FLY OUT

Jackie Jensen was a star slugger for the Boston Red Sox in the 1950's. He recorded more RBIs than anyone else in the American League from 1954-59, and in 1958 he was voted the league's Most Valuable Player. But he quit baseball in 1961, even though he was just 34 years old. Why? Because baseball teams began taking airplanes instead of trains from city to city, and Jackie couldn't conquer his fear of flying!

## WILLIE, MICKEY, AND THE DUKE

One of the biggest arguments in New York in the 1950's was: Who is the city's best centerfielder?

Willie Mays played centerfield for the New York Giants, Mickey Mantle played for the New York Yankees, and Duke Snider played for the Brooklyn Dodgers. In the four full seasons the terrific trio played in New York (1954 to 1957), their statistics were very similar and very, very good!

Over those four seasons, Willie batted .323 and averaged 41 home runs, 114 runs scored, and 105 runs batted in. Mickey batted .331 and averaged 38 homers, 126 runs scored, and 106 RBIs. Finally, Duke batted .304 and averaged 42 homers, 112 runs scored, and 115 RBIs.

Willie's total of 660 home runs is the third most ever, behind only Hank Aaron and Babe Ruth. He had 12 straight seasons in which he scored at least 100 runs, and he is the only man in history to lead the league in home runs and stolen bases four times each.

Mickey also led his league in home runs four times. He hit 52 in 1956 and 54 in 1961. For his career, he had 536 home runs. Mickey led the league in runs scored six times, including 1956. That year, he won the Triple Crown, leading the league in batting average (.353), home runs (52), and RBIs (130). It was one of the greatest seasons any slugger has ever had.

Duke had five straight seasons of 40 or more home runs. He batted .300 or better seven times and finished his career with 407 home runs. Mickey was elected to the Hall of Fame in 1974, Willie was elected in 1979, and Duke made it three-for-three by joining the Hall of Fame in 1980.

## THE TRIPLE CROWN CLUB

Winnning the Triple Crown is one of the most difficult feats in baseball. Only 16 players in history have led their league in batting average, home runs, and RBIs all in the same season. Many of the game's all-time greats never won a Triple Crown, including Babe Ruth, Joe DiMaggio, Willie Mays, and Hank Aaron.

Seven National League players and nine American

League players have done it, but nobody has won the Triple Crown since Boston Red Sox leftfielder Carl Yastrzemski last did it in 1967.

Only two men have done it twice. Rogers Hornsby, a second baseman for the St. Louis Cardinals, did it in 1922 and 1925. He was one of the best sluggers ever to play the game, producing a lifetime batting average of .358, the second best of all time. The only other man to win two Triple Crowns was also one of the game's greatest hitters — Ted Williams. He did it in 1942 and 1947.

But in 1933, an incredible thing happened. There was a Triple Crown winner in each league — and they both played in the same city! Chuck Klein did it in the National League for the Philadelphia Phillies, and Jimmie Foxx did it in the American League for the Philadelphia A's.

## NUTTY NICKNAMES

| | |
|---|---|
| Willie Mays (1951-1973) | "The Say Hey Kid" |
| Camilo Pascual (1954-1971) | "The Little Potato" |
| Harmon Killebrew (1954-1975) | "Killer" |
| Sal Maglie (1945-1958) | "The Barber" |

## IT HAPPENS TO THE BEST OF US

The following eight players are in the Hall of Fame, but here are some records that they wish they hadn't set:

- Hank Aaron — set a record by hitting into 328 double plays in his career.
- Lou Brock — was thrown out stealing a record 307 times.
- Ty Cobb — committed more errors (275) than any other outfielder.

- Jimmie Foxx — led the A.L. in strikeouts a record seven times.

- Reggie Jackson — struck out 2,597 times.

- Nap Lajoie — once committed five errors in a single game.

- Cy Young — lost 316 games, the most by any pitcher.

- Brooks Robinson — hit into a record four career triple plays.

## EXTRA INNINGS

You've got the "inside pitch" on some of baseball's best moments. Now try answering these questions to see if you've caught on. Check your score on page 72 to find out if you are an MVP or a minor leaguer!

**1.** What are the three categories in which a hitter must lead the league in order to win the Triple Crown?

**2.** Ted Williams is the last major league player to reach the magic .400 mark, hitting .406 in 1941. What major league player has come the closest since then, batting .390 in 1980?

**3.** In 1956, Don Larsen pitched the only perfect game in World Series history, against the Brooklyn Dodgers. What is a perfect game?

**4.** Lou Gehrig set a record by playing in an amazing 2,130 consecutive games. What current big league player has a chance to break that record in a few years?

# THE NATIONAL GAME

Below are 15 superstars and 15 teams. Can you match the player with the team he is known best for playing with? Write the letter of the correct team next to each number on the opposite page. Then, in the space on the right, write in the city that team comes from. The first one, Ryne Sandberg of the Cubs, is done for you. When you're finished, write the circled letters from each city name in order at the bottom of the page and see the name of one of baseball's newest teams. (Check your answers on page 75.)

| | | | |
|---|---|---|---|
| **1.** Ryne Sandberg | **A.** A's |
| **2.** Cal Ripken, Jr. | **B.** Yankees |
| **3.** Sandy Koufax | **C.** Mariners |
| **4.** Lou Gehrig | **D.** Dodgers |
| **5.** Cecil Fielder | **E.** Pirates |
| **6.** Mark McGwire | **F.** Reds |
| **7.** Tony Gwynn | **G.** Orioles |
| **8.** Ted Williams | **H.** Tigers |
| **9.** Willie Mays | **I.** Brewers |
| **10.** Roberto Alomar | **J.** Red Sox |
| **11.** Pete Rose | **K.** Cubs |
| **12.** George Brett | **L.** Padres |
| **13.** Roberto Clemente | **M.** Royals |
| **14.** Robin Yount | **N.** Giants |
| **15.** Ken Griffey, Jr. | **O.** Blue Jays |

1. _K_ (C) H I C A G O
2. _G_ B a l t i m (o) r e
3. _D_ L O S   A N G E (L) E S
4. _B_ N E W   Y (O) R K
5. _H_ D E T R (O) I T
6. _A_ O (A) K L A N D
7. _I_ S A N (D) I E G O
8. _J_ B (O) S T O N
9. _N_ S A N
        (F) R A N S I S C O
10. _O_ T O R (O) N T O
11. _F_ C I N (C) I N N A T I
12. _M_ (K) A N S A S   C I T Y
13. _E_ P (I) T T S B U R G H
14. _I_ M I L W A U K E (E)
15. _C_ (S) E A T T L E

**SECRET TEAM:**
C O L O R A D O
R O C K I E S

39

# WHO STOLE HOME?

You've heard of people stealing home. In this case, somebody stole home plate! The managers and the umpires gathered around home plate at the beginning of the All-Star Game to exchange lineups, and they noticed the plate was missing!

They have to find home plate or they can't play the game. The only clue left behind is a baseball card with the suspect's picture and stats. But the card is so torn up that the umpires couldn't figure out the player's name. All they can get from it is some general information about him.

With the few clues they have and a list of eight suspects, can you figure out who stole home plate? (Check your answer on page 75.)

## THE CLUES:

1. The suspect is at least six feet tall.
2. The suspect hit at least 20 home runs in the previous season.
3. The suspect's uniform is at least partly colored red.
4. The suspect weighs less than 200 pounds
5. The suspect is righthanded.

## THE SUSPECTS:

1. **SAMMY SLUGGER.** Sammy is a designated hitter for the Washington Werewolves, whose team colors are red and brown. He is a righthanded batter who hit 35 home runs. Sammy is 6' 2" and weighs 220 pounds.

40

**2. KNUCKLES NELSON.** Knuckles is a member of the Tampa Tubas, a team with red and gold uniforms. Knuckles is six feet tall and weighs 195 pounds. He is a lefthanded pitcher who has hit only one home run in his career.

**3. GARY GLOVEWORK.** Gary is a shortstop for the Providence Peanuts. He is righthanded and wears a blue and yellow uniform. Gary is six feet tall and weighs 180 pounds. Last season, he hit 12 home runs.

**4. WILLIE WHIFFER.** Willie is a rightfielder for the Indianapolis Inchworms. His uniform is red and white, and he is righthanded. Willie is 6' 3" and weighs 235 pounds. Last season, he hit 27 home runs.

**5. TOMMY GUNN.** Tommy is a catcher for the Santa Fe Spirits, whose uniforms are red and green. Last season, the righthander hit 21 home runs. He is 6' 1" and weighs 190 pounds.

**6. HARRY HOTCORNER.** Harry is a third baseman for the Boise Bullets. He is righthanded, six feet tall, and weighs 195 pounds. Last season, Harry hit 32 home runs. The Bullets wear blue and orange uniforms.

**7. WALTER MITT.** Walter is a first baseman for the Kentucky Curveballs, whose uniforms are purple and red. He is 6' 1" and weighs 180 pounds. Harry hit 22 home runs and is lefthanded.

**8. ABNER DOUBLEPLAY.** Abner is a second baseman for the Portland Peacocks, whose uniforms are green, blue, yellow, and orange. Abner is a 5' 9", 165-pounder. He is a righthander who hit eight home runs.

**THE THIEF IS** Tommy Gunn

# 1960's-1990's

# MODERN TIMES

### 1960 ▷ WORLD SERIES MOMENT

The seventh game of the 1960 World Series was one of the most dramatic games in the history of the Fall Classic. The Pittsburgh Pirates were leading the New York Yankees, 4-0, but the Yankees rebounded to take a 7-4 lead. The Pirates scored five runs in the eighth inning to make it 9-7, and then New York tied the game with two runs in the top of the ninth.

Leading off the bottom of the ninth was Pittsburgh second baseman Bill Mazeroski. Bill was known more for his fielding than for his hitting, and he had hit only 11 homers all season. But he swung at the second pitch and belted it over the leftfield fence for a game-winning homer.

"I was too excited and too thrilled to think," he later said. "It was the greatest moment of my life."

### 1961 ▷ 61 IN '61

When Babe Ruth hit 60 home runs in 1927, people thought the record would last forever. But it lasted only 34 years.

In 1961, New York Yankee rightfielder Roger Maris hit his record-breaking 61st homer on the last day of the season. Roger won the American League Most Valuable Player Award for the second straight season, and the Yankees went

# SANDY KOUFAX

When Sandy Koufax first came up to the majors with the Brooklyn Dodgers in 1955, he threw hard but he didn't throw very well. Six years later, though, he was as good as any pitcher who has played the game.

From 1961 through 1966, he led the National League in earned run average five times, strikeouts four times, and wins three times. He also tossed four no-hitters, a record until Nolan Ryan came along. In 1966, Sandy decided to quit baseball because of a sore elbow, retiring at the top of his game.

NATIONAL BASEBALL LIBRARY, COOPERSTOWN, NY

on to win the World Series.

But Roger couldn't keep up the power. Because of injuries, he played only one more full season in the big leagues, finishing with 275 career home runs. Even though he's the man who hit more homers in a season than anybody else, he is not in the Hall of Fame.

## 1962 NEW YORK MESS

In 1962, a new team arrived in New York called the New York Mets, and they may have been the worst team in baseball history.

The Mets lost 120 games that year, a modern day major league record. They should have known they would have bad luck that year when their first game at home was played on Friday the 13th!

In the Mets' final game — and loss — of the season seldom-used catcher Joe Pignatano was sent to the plate. It was the final at-bat of his big league career, and he hit into a triple play!

## NAME GAME

The 120 losses weren't the only strange thing about the 1962 New York Mets. That year, the Mets had one pitcher named Bob Miller and another named . . . Bob Miller! Both stood 6' 1" and both were righthanded batters. To make matters more confusing, they were roommates on the road!

## OH, BROTHER!

In the 1960's and 1970's, there were three Alou brothers in the major leagues: Felipe, Matty, and Jesus. In 1963, all three Alou brothers were outfielders on the same team, the San Francisco Giants. Years later, the brothers played for another team in California — the Oakland A's — but not at the same time. Felipe, the oldest, played for the A's in 1970 and 1971. Matty, the middle child, played for Oakland in 1972. And Jesus, the youngest, played there in 1973 and 1974. Keeping the family tradition, Felipe now manages the Montreal Expos and his son Moises is one of his players!

### 1965 ▷ NINE LIVES

In 1965, Bert Campaneris of the Kansas City A's became the first player ever to play all nine positions in one game! Three years later, Cesar Tovar of the Minnesota Twins became the second player to do it. He appeared as a pitcher in the first inning, and the first batter he faced was, of all people, Bert Campaneris.

### NO-HIT (AND HIT) MAGIC

Babe Ruth was the best pitcher-hitter combination in baseball history, but for one game at least, two pitchers had similar success both at the plate and on the mound!

On May 9, 1968, Catfish Hunter of the Oakland A's pitched a perfect game against the Minnesota Twins. He also had three hits and four runs batted in.

On June 23, 1971, Rick Wise, the Philadelphia Phillies ace, tossed a no-hitter against the Cincinnati Reds. He also hit two home runs!

### THE YEAR OF THE PITCHER

One thing's for sure — 1968 was not a good year to be a big league hitter. How good were the pitchers that season? Take a look at the stats:

## Wacky Fact

A man named John Miller is the only player in baseball history to homer in his first and last at-bat in the big leagues. The funny thing is, they were the only home runs he hit in his career!

- Denny McLain of the Detroit Tigers became the first major league pitcher in 34 years to win at least 30 games, with a record of 31-6.

- Bob Gibson of the St. Louis Cardinals had the best earned run average in more than half a century — 1.12! He also won 22 games, pitched 13 shutouts, and struck out 35 batters in three World Series games.

- Luis Tiant of the Cleveland Indians led the American League with a 1.60 earned run average and nine shutouts.

- Juan Marichal of the San Francisco Giants pitched 30 complete games and won 26 of them.

- Don Drysdale of the Los Angeles Dodgers pitched 58 consecutive innings without allowing an earned run.

- Carl Yastrzemski of the Boston Red Sox won the A.L. batting crown with a .301 average, the lowest ever for a batting title.

- On April 15, the Houston Astros beat the New York Mets 1-0 in a game that was scoreless until the 24th inning. In all, there were 82 1-0 games during the season.

- The 1968 All-Star Game was also a 1-0 game, and the winning run scored on a double play.

## THE YEAR OF THE McPITCHER

In 1968, three American League pitchers combined for 68 wins, 765 strikeouts, and an ERA under 2.00. Their names were Denny McLain, Dave McNally, and Sam McDowell.

 ## THE AMAZIN' METS

After joining the National League in 1962, the New York Mets were probably the worst team in baseball. They finished in last place five times and in second-to-last place twice in their first seven years. But 1969 would be a different story.

In 1969, two new teams — the Montreal Expos and San Diego Padres — joined the National League. Also, both leagues divided into two divisions, East and West, of six teams each. But that wasn't the only

## HOW TO FIGURE . . . TOTAL BASES

The statistic "total bases" means the number of bases a hitter has covered with his hits. For instance, a home run is worth four bases. A triple is worth three bases, and a double is worth two bases. Singles are worth just one base.

The record for total bases in a game was set by Milwaukee Braves slugger Joe Adcock in 1954. In the game, he had four home runs and one double. How many total bases did he have? (Answer on page 76.)

4 homers x 4 bases = _____
1 double x 2 bases = _____
Total bases = _____

## ROBERTO CLEMENTE

Not only did Pittsburgh Pirate rightfielder Roberto Clemente have one of the strongest arms in baseball history, he was also one of the game's top hitters. Roberto batted over .300 13 times, won four batting titles, and hit .414 when the Pirates won the 1971 World Series.

His last hit of the 1972 regular season was number 3,000 of his career, and would prove to be his last regular season hit ever. After the season, there was a terrible earthquake in the country of Nicaragua. Roberto volunteered to help fly supplies to the survivors, but his plane crashed and his body was never found. He was a great player on the field, but Roberto Clemente will always be remembered as a hero off the field, too.

change in baseball. The New York Mets, led by pitcher Tom Seaver, became winners!

The Chicago Cubs led the Mets by nine and a half games in August, but the Cubs lost 10 of 11 games in early September. At the same time, the Mets went on a tear, winning 38 of 49 games. By the end of the season, the "Amazin' Mets" had won the N.L. East division by eight games!

The Mets beat the Atlanta Braves in the first N.L divisional playoffs — between the N.L. East winner and the N.L. West winner. In the American League, the Baltimore Orioles defeated the Minnesota Twins in the playoffs.

The Orioles had won 109 games that year, and most people thought they would crush the Mets. But, after losing the first game of the World Series, the Mets won four straight. After seven years of being the worst team in baseball, the Mets were world champions!

 **1975**     **OH, BROTHER!**

Brothers Jim and Gaylord Perry were excellent pitchers who won a combined total of 529 games. In 1970, Gaylord led the National League in wins, while Jim led the American League.

Gaylord wound up with almost 100 more career wins than his older brother and was

## WaCKy FaCT

On September 15, 1971, Houston Astro pitcher Larry Yount made his first big league appearance, in the ninth inning against the Atlanta Braves. He threw one pitch, hurt his arm, and never pitched in the majors again!

eventually elected to the Hall of Fame. But for four days in 1975 — from September 22 to September 25 — both Perry brothers had career records of 215 wins and 174 losses. Exactly the same!

## MR. OCTOBER

Reggie Jackson was one of baseball's all-time greatest sluggers. He led the American League in home runs four times and hit 563 in his career. But it was in the World Series that Reggie truly shined.

Reggie played in five World Series — two with the Oakland A's and three with the New York Yankees. In 98 World Series at-bats, he had 35 hits for a .357 batting average. He also scored 21 runs, had 24 runs batted in, and slugged 10 homers.

In the 1977 World Series, Reggie's New York Yankees defeated the Los Angeles Dodgers. Reggie belted a record five home runs in the six-game Series, including three in the final game. The only other player to hit three homers in a World Series game is Babe Ruth, but Reggie hit them on three consecutive pitches!

Since the World Series always takes place in October, the world knew exactly what to call Reggie Jackson — Mr. October.

## BROTHER VS. BROTHER

On May 31, 1979, rookie pitcher Pat Underwood of the Detroit Tigers played his first game in the major leagues. The starting pitcher on the opposing team was his older brother, Tom! Naturally, it turned out to be a pitchers' duel. The rookie beat his older brother, 1-0.

# HANK AARON

If you take all the players who have ever played major league baseball, and put them in alphabetical order, Hank Aaron comes first. And he deserves to be there, as he comes in first in other ways as well.

On April 8, 1974, Hank hit his 715th home run, one more than the immortal Babe Ruth. It was a record that few people thought would ever be broken, but "Hammerin' Hank" finished with 755 homers in his 23-year career. He also had a .305 lifetime batting average and a record 2,297 runs batted in.

Some day, some time, somebody may hit more home runs than Hank Aaron. But until then, he'll always be known as the "Home Run King."

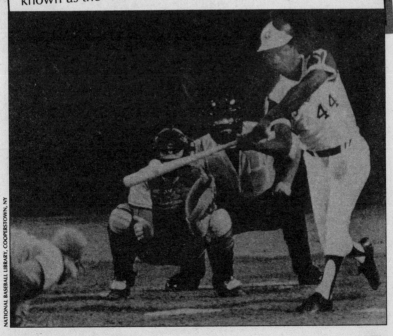

## THE 3,000-HIT CLUB

It's not easy getting 3,000 hits in a career: Only 19 major league players have done it! It means getting 200 hits each season for at least 15 seasons.

In fact, the list of players who never reached the exclusive 3,000-hit club includes some of the best players in major league history — sluggers like Babe Ruth, Lou Gehrig, Joe DiMaggio, Ted Williams, and Mickey Mantle. Here's the list of players who did make the club:

| | | |
|---|---|---|
| 1. | Pete Rose | 4,256 |
| 2. | Ty Cobb | 4,191 |
| 3. | Hank Aaron | 3,771 |
| 4. | Stan Musial | 3,630 |
| 5. | Tris Speaker | 3,514 |
| 6. | Carl Yastrzemski | 3,419 |
| 7. | Honus Wagner | 3,418 |
| 8. | Eddie Collins | 3,313 |
| 9. | Willie Mays | 3,283 |
| 10. | Nap Lajoie | 3,244 |
| 11. | Paul Waner | 3,152 |
| 12. | Robin Yount | 3,142 |
| 13. | George Brett | 3,154 |
| 14. | Rod Carew | 3,053 |
| 15. | Lou Brock | 3,023 |
| 16. | Dave Winfield | 3,014 |
| 17. | Al Kaline | 3,007 |

18. Cap Anson 3,000   19. Roberto Clemente 3,000

**HIT MAN**

On August 4, 1982, Joel Youngblood collected two hits — for two different teams — the only player ever to do that!

Joel started the day playing for the New York Mets, and he had a hit in a day game against the Chicago Cubs. After the game, he was traded from the Mets to the Montreal Expos. He flew to Philadelphia to play with the Expos against the Phillies that night. In his only at-bat of the game, he hit a single!

## RUNNIN' RICKEY

Rickey Henderson is the greatest base stealer of all-time. In 1982, Rickey set a major league record by stealing 130 bases for the Oakland A's. Less than 10 years later, he passed Lou Brock to become the all-time stolen base leader. Today, he is the only player ever to steal more than 1,000 bases in his career.

But Rickey isn't only a base stealer. In his career, he has hit 220 home runs. In fact, he has set an unusual record by leading off a game by hitting a home run 63 times in his career!

 **ACT YOUR AGE**

"K" is the symbol for a strikeout when you're keeping score on a scorecard, so it's no wonder that New York Mets pitcher Dwight Gooden was given the nickname "Dr. K."

In 1985, Dwight led the National League with 24 wins, 268 strikeouts, and a terrific 1.53 earned run average. And at age 20, he became the youngest pitcher to ever win the Cy Young Award, and the youngest to be the strikeout leader!

## HAPPY FIFTH OF JULY!

On the night of July 4, 1985, the Atlanta Braves and the New York Mets played a game that lasted 19 innings. After more than six hours of play, including a 90-minute rain delay, the game ended with the Mets winning, 16-13, at 3:55

## THE 500-HOMER CLUB

There's an easy way to assure yourself a spot in the Baseball Hall of Fame. Just hit 500 home runs!

Only 14 players have ever done it, and they are 14 of the greatest sluggers ever to play the game. To hit 500 homers, a player has to average 25 home runs a year for 20 years. To hit 755 career home runs, as Hank Aaron did, you have to average more than 37 home runs a year for 20 years.

The first person to reach 500 home runs was New York Yankee star Babe Ruth, who smashed his 500th in 1929. The last person to reach the 500-homer club was Philadelphia Phillies third baseman Mike Schmidt, who did it in 1987.

Here's a list of all of baseball's home run kings:
1. Hank Aaron (755)
2. Babe Ruth (714)
3. Willie Mays (660)
4. Frank Robinson (586)
5. Harmon Killebrew (573)
6. Reggie Jackson (563)
7. Mike Schmidt (548)
8. Mickey Mantle (536)
9. Jimmie Foxx (534)
10. Ted Williams (521)
    Willie McCovey (521)
12. Eddie Mathews (512)
    Ernie Banks (512)
14. Mel Ott (511)

the following morning.

Even though it was really July 5, it was finally time for the postgame Fourth of July fireworks!

## ROCKET ROGER

Boston Red Sox star Roger Clemens is one of the best pitchers in baseball. In fact, he's been one of the best ever since he joined the big leagues in 1984.

In 1986, his first full season in the majors, "The Rocket" led the American League with a record of 24-4 and a 2.48 ERA. He won the A.L. Cy Young Award, the first of three he has won in his career.

But the highlight of his season came on April 29. In a 3-1 victory over the Seattle Mariners, Roger struck out 20 batters — a big league record!

## BIG BLOOPER

The Boston Red Sox hadn't won the World Series since 1918, but in 1986 they were just one game away from a world championship. The Red Sox led the New York Mets three games to two, and their best pitcher — Roger Clemens — was starting Game 6.

The game went into extra innings tied at 3-3, and Boston needed to score one run to win the Series. They got that run in the top of the 10th inning when Dave Henderson hit a home run, and Wade Boggs added an insurance run by scoring after hitting a double. Fans all over Boston began to celebrate, and the scoreboard operator at New York's Shea Stadium even accidentally flashed the words "CONGRATU-LATIONS BOSTON RED SOX" on the scoreboard before the game had ended.

But the Mets still had one last chance in the bottom of the 10th inning. New York's first two batters flied out, so the Mets were down to their last out. Was it possible? Would the Red Sox finally win a World Series for the first time in 68 years?

No.

Gary Carter and pinch hitter Kevin Mitchell each slapped singles for the Mets. Then Ray Knight's single scored Gary and a wild pitch scored Kevin. It was 5-5 with two outs and a runner on second base. With a full count, Mookie Wilson hit a ground ball to Boston first baseman Bill Buckner . . . and it went between his legs!

Knight scored the winning run, and two days later, the Mets won Game 7 to take the World Series. And Bill Buckner? He was an excellent player for 22 years in the big leagues, but his big blooper will never be forgotten.

## NUTTY NICKNAMES

| | |
|---|---|
| Carlton Fisk (1969-1993) | "Pudge" |
| Greg Luzinski (1970-1984) | "The Bull" |
| Ron Cey (1971-1987) | "Penguin" |
| Rick Burleson (1974-1987) | "Rooster" |

### 1988 ▷ WORLD SERIES MOMENT

Two stars of the Los Angeles Dodgers produced fantastic finishes in 1988. Pitcher Orel Hershiser won 23 games that year and finished the season by pitching an amazing 59 scoreless innings in a row. That broke the record Don Drysdale set for the same team exactly 20 years earlier — by one inning!

Orel won the National League Cy Young Award, and

he was also the World Series MVP. In the Series, he won two games, and the Dodgers beat the favored Oakland A's.

But the N. L. Most Valuable Player in 1988 was another Dodger star — Kirk Gibson. In the first game of the World Series, he produced one of the most dramatic and exciting moments in baseball history.

Kirk had injured his leg, so he sat out most of that first game. But with the Dodgers trailing, 4-3, two outs in the bottom of the ninth, and a man on base, Kirk was sent in to pinch hit against relief ace Dennis Eckersley. He limped up to the plate and smashed a two-run homer over the rightfield fence to give the Dodgers a 5-4 victory and send them on their way to a world championship.

## THE OTHER GREAT THIRD BASEMAN

While Mike Schmidt was winning the 1980 MVP Award in the National League (see next page), another third baseman was winning it in the American League. His name is George Brett, and he was also one of the greatest third basemen in history.

George led the American League in hitting in 1976, batting .333. In 1980, the Kansas City Royal slugger was even better, finishing with an amazing .390 batting average. All season, he threatened to become the first player to bat .400 since Ted Williams did it in 1941. Ten years later, in 1990, George won a third batting title, at the age of 37, with an average of .329. That made him the first player ever to win batting titles in three different decades!

In 1992, Brett joined the 3,000-hit club, and he retired from baseball at the end of 1993. Someday he's sure to be elected to the Hall of Fame.

# MIKE SCHMIDT

Mike Schmidt retired from baseball on May 29, 1989, but he was so good that the fans paid him the ultimate tribute: They still selected him to appear in the 1989 All-Star Game! He was well-loved in Philadelphia, playing for the Phillies his entire 18-year career.

When Mike played his first full season in the majors in 1973, he wasn't very successful. He batted only .196 and struck out 136 times. But Mike went on to hit 548 home runs, win three N.L. MVP awards, and earn 10 Gold Gloves for his fielding. As a complete player, there was never a better third baseman than Mike Schmidt.

RONALD C. MODRA

**A SAD YEAR FOR BASEBALL**

There have certainly been happier years in baseball than the 1989 season. It was a year of sad and disappointing events.

In August, Cincinnati Red manager Pete Rose was banned from baseball for life because of his involvement with gambling. Pete is baseball's all-time hit leader with a total of 4,256, but baseball has had strict rules against gambling since the Black Sox Scandal of 1919 (see page 11). It was decided thatin his gambling activities, Pete "was not acting in the best interests of baseball." A short time later, on September 1, baseball commissioner Bart Giamatti died of a heart attack, which only added to the sadness.

The scariest moment in baseball in 1989 came at 5:04 p.m. on October 17 in San Francisco's Candlestick Park. The San Francisco Giants and Oakland A's were getting ready to play the third game of the World Series. Suddenly, the fans and players felt a tremor in the stadium. It was an earthquake!

Though the stadium was not damaged and no fans or players were hurt, the earthquake caused billions of dollars of damage to the city of San Francisco. Many people died in the city's worst earthquake in more than 80 years. Fay Vincent, who had taken over for Bart Giamatti as the baseball commissioner, decided to postpone the World Series until the city got back on its feet. Ten days later, Game 3 was finally played, but everybody realized that helping the community during a disaster was much more important than playing a baseball game.

## LIKE FATHER, LIKE SON

Ken Griffey, Jr. is one of baseball's best players in the 1990's. His father — Ken Griffey, Sr. — was one of baseball's best players in the 1970's and 1980's. In 1989, while Ken Jr. was just starting his career with the Seattle Mariners, Ken Sr. was still playing. That made them the first father-son combination to play in the major leagues at the same time!

One year later, in September, father and son became teammates on the Mariners! One game, they hit back-to-back home runs, another baseball first for a father and son!

## BIG AND TALL

Seattle Mariner pitcher Randy Johnson has thrown two no-hitters in his career, maybe because he strikes fear in opposing batters. After all, at 6' 10", Randy is one of the two tallest players in major league history. (Met pitcher Eric Hillman is the other also at 6'10".) Randy joined the Mariners in 1989, but he wasn't the biggest thrower the team saw that year. Before the Opening Day game between Seattle and Oakland, the A's had an even bigger hurler throw out the first ball — an elephant!

## 1990 ANNOUNCER'S NIGHTMARE

In a game between the Montreal Expos and the Philadelphia Phillies on June 13, 1990, Montreal's Dennis Martinez pitched to Philadelphia's Carmelo Martinez, who hit a fly ball that was caught by centerfielder Dave Martinez.

## NO-HIT MAGIC

In 1990, Detroit Tiger first baseman Cecil Fielder became only the 18th player ever to hit 50 or more home

# THE 30-30 CLUB

The 30-30 club honors players who combine strength and speed. To join it, a player has to hit 30 homers and steal 30 bases in the same season. In baseball history, only 14 players have done it.

The first person to reach 30-30 was Ken Williams of the St. Louis Browns, who hit 39 homers and stole 37 bases way back in 1922. No one else joined the club for another 33 years! In 1988, Jose Canseco of the Oakland A's hit 42 home runs and stole 40 bases, making him the only member of the 40-40 club! Here's a list of the members of the 30-30 club, and the years in which each player performed the feat.

Ken Williams (1922)
Willie Mays (1956, 1957)
Hank Aaron (1963)
Bobby Bonds (1969, 1973, 1975, 1977, 1978)
Tommy Harper (1970)
Dale Murphy (1983)
Joe Carter (1987)
Eric Davis (1987)
Darryl Strawberry (1987)
Howard Johnson (1987, 1989, 1991)
Jose Canseco (1988)
Ron Gant (1990, 1991)
Barry Bonds (1990, 1992)
Sammy Sosa (1993)

runs in a season, Chicago White Sox Carlton Fisk set a record by hitting his 329th home run as a catcher, and Oakland A's Rickey Henderson broke Lou Brock's record for most career stolen bases.

But the most amazing thing about 1990 was the number of no-hitters. For the first time in baseball history, there were eight no-hitters thrown in one season!

Not only were there a lot of them, but there were all kinds of no-hitters, too. For example, on April 11, Mark Langston and Mike Witt of the California Angels combined to throw a no-hitter. And on June 2, Randy Johnson — the 6' 10" pitcher for the Seattle Mariners — became the tallest pitcher ever to throw a no-hitter.

On June 29, two pitchers in different leagues threw no-hitters on the same day. Dave Stewart of the Oakland A's did it, and then later that day Fernando Valenzuela of the Los Angeles Dodgers did it, too. But perhaps the most impressive no-hitter of them all happened on June 11, the day 43-year-old Nolan Ryan of the Texas Rangers became the oldest man to toss a no-hitter. Not only did Nolan lead the league in strikeouts in 1990, but he also won his 300th career game.

## NUTTY NICKNAMES

| | |
|---|---|
| Frank Thomas | "The Big Hurt" |
| Ryne Sandberg | "Ryno" |
| Lenny Dykstra | "Nails" |
| Ozzie Smith | "Wizard of Oz" |

## DOUBLE TRIPLE

On July 17, 1990, the Minnesota Twins did something no other team has ever done. They made two triple plays in

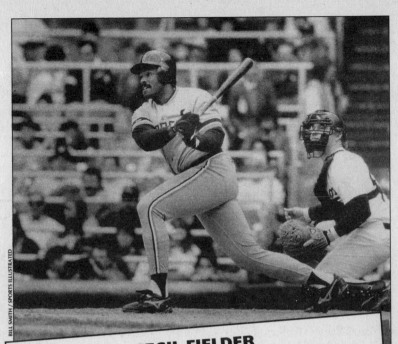

BILL SMITH / SPORTS ILLUSTRATED

## CECIL FIELDER

Cecil Fielder wasn't too happy during his first four seasons in the big leagues. As a member of the Toronto Blue Jays from 1985-88, he couldn't get into the starting lineup. So in 1989 he decided to play baseball in Japan, where his towering home runs made him very popular.

That's when the Detroit Tigers noticed the big slugger and signed him up for the 1990 season. Cecil responded by hitting 51 home runs, the most in the American League in nearly 30 years. Cecil hit 44 homers in 1991 and 35 in 1992. In 1993, he belted 30 home runs. Over his first four full major league seasons, he had a total of 506 runs batted in! From 1990-1992, Cecil led the American League in RBIs each season. The last person to do that was a man named Babe Ruth. Not bad company!

one game!

## BONDS AND MORE BONDS

Bobby Bonds is the undisputed king of the 30-30 club. He performed the feat five times in his career — for five different teams!

Now Bobby's son, Barry, is a star leftfielder for the San Francisco Giants. Barry, who is one of the best players in baseball, may be on his way to collecting a handful of 30-30 seasons. He has two 30-30 seasons already!

Will he be able to catch his father? Stay tuned.

## RYNO

Chicago Cub second baseman Ryne Sandberg is not only one of the greatest defensive second basemen of all time, he's also an offensive superstar. While winning nine straight Gold Gloves for fielding excellence from 1983-91, Ryne put up some hitting and baserunning numbers that few players have matched.

In 1985, Ryne stole 54 bases. In 1990, he hit 40 home runs. That makes him one of only two players (Barry Bonds is the other) ever to hit at least 40 homers and steal at least 50 bases in separate seasons.

## 1990   BIG BLOOPER

On April 30, 1990, New York Met pitcher David Cone showed what can happen when you argue with an umpire. The Mets were playing the Atlanta Braves, and a ground ball was hit to Met first baseman Mike Marshall. He flipped the ball to David, who was covering first base, but umpire Charlie Williams called the runner safe. He said David's foot hadn't touched the base.

David couldn't believe it. He began arguing . . . and arguing . . . and arguing. He forgot to watch the runners on second and third base. While he was protesting the call, both runners came around to score!

The Mets lost the game, 7-4, and afterward New York manager Davey Johnson said, "I've seen some strange things in my life in baseball, but this is up there at the top of the list."

## 1991 ▷ WORLD SERIES MOMENT

The 1991 World Series between the Minnesota Twins and the Atlanta Braves was certainly one of the most exciting Series ever. There were five one-run games, four games won on the very last play, and three extra-inning games.

In Game 6, Minnesota's Kirby Puckett had one of the best nights any player has ever had in a World Series. After nine innings, Kirby had a single, a triple, a sacrifice fly, a run, and a stolen base, and he had made a great catch in centerfield. The game went into extra innings. So what did he do in the 11th inning? He hit the game-winning home run. The Twins won Game 7 as well to become world champions.

## WaCKy FaCT

Minnesota Twin slugger Kirby Puckett went 5,129 at-bats from the start of his career without hitting a grand slam. But he finally hit one on May 29, 1992. Then he hit a second grand slam later that week and a third later that season!

## HIGH POP FLY

On May 30, 1992, Detroit Tigers slugger Rob Deer twice hit pop-ups so high that they bounced off the ceiling of the Hubert H. Humphrey Metrodome in Minneapolis. Both times, Minnesota Twins shortstop Greg Gagne caught them for the out!

## ACT YOUR AGE

In 1992, Dave Winfield of the Toronto Blue Jays became the oldest man ever to have at least 100 RBIs in a season, collecting 108 at the age of 40. Even the best baseball players start to fade once they reach their late 30's, and most are retired by the time they're 40. But some, like Dave, keep going after most players are long gone. Here's a list of some "oldies but goodies":

- Dave Winfield (1992, age 40) — 26 home runs, 108 runs batted in
- Nolan Ryan (1987, age 40) — led the N.L. with 2.76 ERA and 270 strikeouts
- Pete Rose (1981, age 40) — batted .325 and led the league with 140 hits
- Sam Rice (1930, age 40) — .349 with 207 hits and 121 runs scored
- Ty Cobb (1927, age 40) — batted .357 with 104 runs scored and 93 RBIs
- Darrell Evans (1987, age 40) — 34 homers and 99 RBIs
- Ted Williams (1960, age 41) — .316 with 29 home runs
- Stan Musial (1962, age 41) — .330 with 19 homers and 82 RBIs

- Cy Young (1908, age 41) — 21-11 record, 1.26 ERA
- Hoyt Wilhelm (1964, age 41) — 12-9, 1.99 ERA, 27 saves
- Warren Spahn (1963, age 42) — 23-7, 2.60 ERA
- Phil Niekro (1982, age 43) — 17-4, .810 winning percentage

## THE WIZARD OF OZ

Ozzie Smith of the St. Louis Cardinals is regarded as perhaps the greatest defensive shortstop in baseball history. Ozzie won 13 straight Gold Gloves from 1980-92. No other shortstop has ever won that many. In fact, 1992 was a milestone year for Ozzie in several ways. It was the year he recorded his 2,000th hit, his 7,000th assist, and his 500th stolen base.

## NAME GAME

It happened in a three-game series between the Houston Astros and the Philadelphia Phillies from May 29-31, 1992. Philadelphia's Barry Jones was the winning pitcher in the first and third games. In the second game, Houston's Jimmy Jones got the win and Doug Jones picked up a save.

## 1993 ▷ USING HIS HEAD

On May 26, 1993, Carlos Martinez of the Cleveland Indians hit a deep fly ball toward rightfielder Jose Canseco of the Texas Rangers. Canseco went back to catch the ball, but he misjudged it. The ball bounced off the top of his head and over the fence for a home run!

## BO KNOWS BASEBALL

Before he injured his hip while playing professional football, Bo Jackson combined power and speed as well as anybody. After winning the 1985 Heisman Trophy as the top college football player in the country, Bo decided to try playing major league baseball. Four years later, he was a Kansas City Royal, playing in the All-Star Game, and he led off the game with a towering home run!

Bo's hip injury ended his football career. After being fitted with an artificial hip, he told the world he would return to professional baseball. Few people believed he could. After all, nobody had ever played pro baseball with an artificial hip.

But wouldn't you know it, Bo made it back. In his first at-bat (with the Chicago White Sox in 1993), he hit a home run!

## WINLESS

Anthony Young is certainly no Cy Young. Cy Young has the record for most wins (511) in a career, but in 1993 Anthony Young set a major league record for most consecutive losses.

Anthony, a pitcher for the New York Mets, began his streak on May 6, 1992. He lost that day, and he kept on losing. Although he often pitched well during the streak, he and his team couldn't seem to get a victory to stop the slide. By the time the streak ended on July 28, 1993, Anthony had suffered through 27 consecutive losses!

## A TRUE HERO

In 1988, the California Angels drafted a pitcher from

the University of Michigan, making him the eighth pick in the nation. This pitcher had received the Sullivan Award as the nation's top amateur athlete even though he was born without a right hand! But Jim Abbott was special. In fact, on September 4, 1993, he pitched a no-hitter for the New York Yankees.

# EXTRA INNINGS

Last licks! Take a swing at these questions for a real test of your baseball brain. Check your score on page 72 to see if you are an MVP or a minor leaguer!

**1.** Bo Jackson has played professional baseball with the Kansas City Royals and the Chicago White Sox. What professional football team did he play for?

**2.** Nolan Ryan set a record by striking out 383 batters in 1973. Whose record did he break?

**3.** Felipe, Matty, and Jesus Alou were all teammates on the San Francisco Giants in 1963. Which one of them manages the Montreal Expos today, the team on which his son, Moises, plays?

**4.** Kirk Gibson's dramatic home run in Game 1 of the 1988 World Series was hit off one of the best relief pitchers in the American League. Can you name him?

# EIGHT-BALL

Can you take the last names of each of the eight baseball players below and write them from top to bottom in their proper columns in the grid on the next page? The word BASEBALL will help you figure out where certain letters should go. The first one is done for you.

Once you've filled in all the names, write the letters from the shaded boxes in the scrambled name spaces under the grid. Unscramble those letters to get the eight-letter last name of another current baseball star who may someday be in the Hall of Fame. (Check your answers on page 76.)

Chris SABO

~~Barry BONDS~~

Roberto ALOMAR

John OLERUD

Bobby BONILLA

Roger CLEMENS

Mark LANGSTON

Matt WILLIAMS

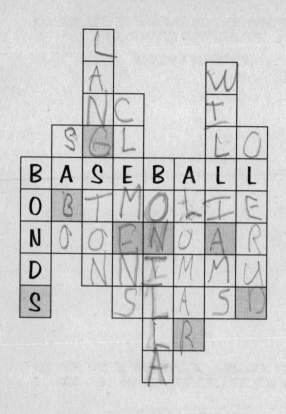

**Scrambled name**

S B G E N R A O

**Unscrambled name**

S A N D B E R G

# EXTRA INNINGS ANSWERS:

## 1900's-1920's

1. The New York Yankees
2. Cy Young
3. Pete Rose
4. The Washington Senators

## 1930's-1950's

1. Batting average, home runs, and runs batted in
2. George Brett
3. In a perfect game, the pitcher allows *no* baserunners.
4. Cal Ripken, Jr.

## 1960's-1990's

1. Los Angeles Raiders
2. Sandy Koufax
3. Felipe Alou
4. Dennis Eckersley

# EXTRA INNINGS SCOREBOARD

| If you get: | You are: |
| --- | --- |
| 4 OUT OF 4 CORRECT | AN MVP |
| 3 OUT OF 4 CORRECT | AN ALL-STAR |
| 2 OUT OF 4 CORRECT | A HOT ROOKIE |
| 1 OUT OF 4 CORRECT | A MINOR LEAGUER |
| 0 OUT OF 4 CORRECT | WAY OFF BASE |

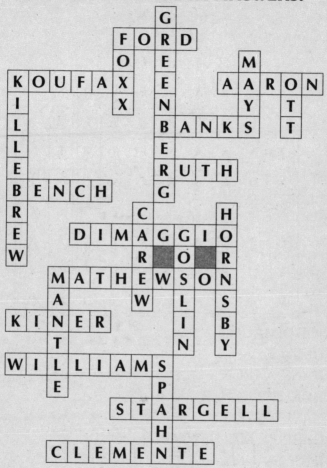

# SIBLING SCRAMBLE ANSWERS:

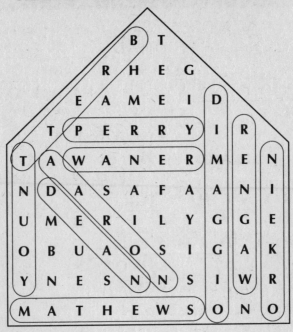

1. JOE DIMAGGIO
2. DIZZY DEAN
3. HANK AARON
4. HONUS WAGNER
5. GAYLORD PERRY
6. CHRISTY MATHEWSON
7. PAUL WANER
8. PHIL NIEKRO
9. GEORGE BRETT
10. ROBIN YOUNT

**SECRET PHRASE:** The game is a family business.

# THE NATIONAL GAME ANSWERS:

1. K    CHICAGO
2. G    BALTIMORE
3. D    LOS ANGELES
4. B    NEW YORK
5. H    DETROIT
6. A    OAKLAND
7. L    SAN DIEGO
8. J    BOSTON
9. N    SAN FRANCISCO
10. O    TORONTO
11. F    CINCINNATI
12. M    KANSAS CITY
13. E    PITTSBURGH
14. I    MILWAUKEE
15. C    SEATTLE

**SECRET TEAM:** COLORADO ROCKIES

## WHO STOLE HOME?

**ANSWER:** TOMMY GUNN

## EIGHT-BALL ANSWERS:

**Scrambled name:**
SBGENRAD

**Unscrambled name:**
SANDBERG

```
      L
      A          W
      N  C       I
   S  G  L       L  O
B  A  S  E  B  A  L  L
O  B  T  M  O  L  I  E
N  O  O  E  N  O  A  R
D     N  N  I  M  M  U
S        S  L  A  S  D
            L  R
            A
```

# HOW TO FIGURE ANSWERS:

### Page 16
Batting Average: 248 divided by 591 = **.4196** which you would round up to **.420**. That's quite an average!

### Page 28
Earned Run Average: 783 divided by 197 = **3.97**

### Page 47
Total Bases:    4 homers x 4 bases = 16
                1 double x 2 bases = 2
                _____
                **18 total bases**

Brad Herzog is a regular contributor to *Sports Illustrated For Kids*. He has written several articles for the magazine and numerous "Play-by-Play" puzzles. A 1990 graduate of Cornell University, Brad was a sports reporter for the *Ithaca Journal* in Ithaca, New York. Now a free-lance writer in Chicago, Brad is also the author of *Heads Up! Puzzles for Sports Brains*, a *Sports Illustrated For Kids* puzzle book. When he's not writing articles or creating puzzles, Brad can be found rooting for his hometown Chicago White Sox.